Basics of Business Mana

Booklet 2

Organisations – the basic units of business

(Where the action is)

A.S. Srinivasan

Clever Fox
PUBLISHING

Chennai • Bangalore

CLEVER FOX PUBLISHING
Chennai, India

Published by CLEVER FOX PUBLISHING 2023
Copyright © A.S.Srinivasan 2023

All Rights Reserved.
ISBN: 978-93-56482-18-0

Organisations - the basic units of business

*Based on my booklet **A Concise Guide to Basics of Business Management**, I thought it would be appropriate to outline major concepts and practices under each functional area as well as business strategy in greater detail in the form of booklets. Thus, along with the Concise Guide, these booklets will give a more detailed coverage of these concepts in the field of business management.*

Of course, each concept in itself has been covered and discussed in great detail by many scholars and there are innumerable books on each of them. No one small booklet like this one, can claim to do justice to all of them in a few pages. This is just a distilled and brief outline of them which again is intended to give an overview of these classic concepts so that the reader becomes familiar with them.

*I have reproduced my Introduction, References and Afterword from my booklet **A Concise Guide to Basics of Business Management** since these booklets will also serve the same purpose to the same audience and are from the same sources. Nothing stated here are original and are based entirely on the materials mentioned in Introduction. I was fortunate to have had the opportunity to study them. Where necessary, I have taken the liberty of using them to preserve their meaning. The errors and misunderstandings are purely result of my limited knowledge and exposure.*

***Booklet 2** in this series is on **Organisations – the basic units of business**. Some of the major aspects of business organisations covered are: How organisations are created, Culture, structure, systems and processes of an organisation and finally Basics of business strategy that enables the organisation to meet its objectives. My fond hope is that this booklet helps you in getting a deeper understanding of the concepts and practices covered and leads you to go further, for in-depth study on topics of your choice.*

A.S. Srinivasan   **October, 2022**

A Concise Guide to Basics of Business Management

Introduction

This booklet will be of use to all those who are interested in the field of Business Management. If you are a practising manager or an entrepreneur, this could serve as a refresher. If you have recently taken up a managerial position, this will be a useful reference book for you to look at some of the concepts mentioned here. If you are a student or a person interested to know the basics of management, this will serve the purpose of a guidebook.

This booklet is brief but comprehensive, outlining all the major management concepts and practices in all functional areas. As a manager in today's highly competitive and dynamic business environment, you need to

1. Develop the capability to look at your organisation's business holistically

2. Become familiar with major concepts and practices in all functional areas of management

3. Understand the integrated nature of your business, the interconnectedness of various functions and the impact of your individual and departmental decisions and actions on the total operations of the company and

4. Have the urge to develop yourself further to meet the challenges of today and tomorrow

Hopefully, this booklet will help you embark on this journey of life-long learning.

I have primarily relied on various management books by leading authors in compiling all the concepts presented here which I *gratefully acknowledge. I claim no originality or ownership of these ideas. I have gathered these over the years I was serving in academics. I have appended a list of primary references and have mentioned the names of original thinkers and writers in my text at appropriate places. There are many more that are in public domain which I have used in presenting these contents.*

All these classic concepts have been mentioned very briefly and need further study for greater understanding. This is in no way a textbook. It is just a window to the field of management. This booklet will have served its purpose if it arouses your curiosity to know more on any topic or concept you are interested in. I look forward to receiving your comments and feedback.

Welcome to a short journey through this fascinating field of management!

A.S. Srinivasan   **October, 2022**

Organisations – the basic units of business

In Booklet 1 titled "Introduction to Business and Management", we first defined what we mean by Business and Management in broad terms. We then moved on to look at the components of business model and, what managers ought to do and what they actually do. Finally, we closed with an overview of how organisations create value, make profits and add on to the wealth of promoters, taking into consideration expectations of other stakeholders as well.

In this booklet, we will be covering the following topics in greater detail:

1. Basics of business organisations

2. Organisational culture, structure, systems and processes

3. Business strategy

We will be using the terms firm, company, enterprise, business, organisation and corporation interchangeably.

1. Organisation basics:

1.1 People make organisations:

People join together to perform their individual activities based on their common objectives, which are co-ordinated to deliver expected results, thus creating an organisation. Hence, we can say that the purposes and goals of the organisation are defined by its people. An organisation can work effectively only when needs of individuals are fulfilled.

1.2 Structure and processes:

We define organisations in terms of their structure and processes. Since organisations bring people together, they need to have a structure in place to carry out the tasks in a co-ordinated manner. Organisational processes are developed over a period of time to define how each task is to be done. There are both formal and informal structures and processes.

1.3 Differentiation and integration:

The two main challenges in managing organisations are:

i. How to differentiate and then integrate? Since individuals will be carrying out the tasks assigned to them, management involves breaking down the jobs to be done and assigning them to individual employees and departments by matching the requirements of the job with skills and knowledge of individuals. This is called differentiation. Management then co-ordinates and integrates all these activities to achieve the desired common objectives. This is integration. While individuals by themselves cannot achieve the company's objectives, this process of differentiation and integration enables people to achieve them by co-ordinating individual efforts and bringing in synergy which means to say that the sum total of individual efforts is greater than mere sum of individual efforts.

    This process of differentiation and integration presents its own challenges. Apart from the problems involved in designing individual jobs and assigning them to suitable individuals, co-ordinating and integrating present greater problems as we shall be seeing in a minute.

ii. Organisation's identity: The second challenge is in building the company's distinct identity through establishing an over-arching purpose and goals for the organisation and striving to achieve them by directing and controlling interactions among the members.

1.4 The "silos" mentality:

When the activities are broken down, they are assigned to departments or sub-units within the organisation. Often, this leads to "silos" mentality which means that individual sub-units work only to fulfil their targets without considering the overall objectives of the company. While some degree of inter-departmental competition will help tone up the system, many times this proves to be dysfunctional. This poses a real challenge to the top management in integrating them to create synergy and achieve the overall objectives. The business world is full of such sub-optimal organisations which have gone in for more and more differentiation with several specialists working in their own silos.

1.5 Organisational designs and structures:

This leads us to the emergence of new organisational designs and structures. In the past, when the jobs and relationships were simple and direct, we had a highly structured, pyramidal and hierarchical bureaucracy. The top boss gave clear and often one-word order- "Do this" or "Don't do this" and this was carried out by his/her immediate sub-ordinates and percolated down the many layers. The underlying management style was "command and control" and there were explicitly stated strict rules, regulations and processes for each job. Individuals just carried out the routine tasks and orders of higher-ups. Those were the days of sellers' markets with scarce means and resources. The central aim of management was to increase the efficiency. These structures flow out of German sociologist, Max Weber's theory of bureaucracy.

But as competition grew and markets turned to be dominated by buyers with different needs and wants, problems and challenges became complex and companies had to differentiate various jobs and co-ordination and integration became a real challenge. The result is today's delayered organisations where number of levels is reduced and decision making delegated to lower levels where the action is, paving the way for self-managed teams.

Further as we will see later, outsourcing has become the order of the day with companies concentrating only on core activities in-house and sub-contracting other activities to suppliers for whom these are their primary activities. Thus, parent organisations have become networked organisations with their suppliers, distributors etc. This has blurred organisational boundaries and these "value chains" from raw material suppliers to finished product distributors to customers compete with one another, in creating and delivering value to customers. With growth of internet leading to interactions between organisation and its customers, even customers participate in the process of value creation, becoming co-creators of value.

1.6 Factors affecting organisational design:

As we saw earlier, organisational design involves differentiation and integration which is the primary responsibility of top management. This involves breaking down the tasks to be performed for achievement of company's objectives and grouping them into individual jobs, sections and departments and then bringing them all together so that tangible end-results are produced. However, each organisation even within the same industry or of similar size, is designed in unique way. Factors that influence organisational design are:

i.   Size of the company: In small organisations with limited number of people, several related tasks will be grouped under one job role. In large organisations, opposite is true.

Volume of work to be carried out will be large and also there will be variety of jobs, calling for services of several specialists.

ii. Life cycle: At birth, companies will be small and more informal with a few jobs and employees performing all tasks. As the organisation grows, the tendency is to "put on fat", adding on jobs, layers, systems and processes.

iii. Technology used: This also decides the design. It is obvious that a high-tech company will employ fewer people while automating several jobs.

iv. Managerial style and beliefs of promoters and senior managers: As discussed earlier, depending on this factor, organisational design may be pyramidal with number of layers or flat with a few levels. Also depending on basic beliefs and decisions on in-house vs. outsourcing, they may become networked organisations with several members in the network.

2. Organisational culture:

2.1 Organisation culture:

We will now move on to the "invisible" but omnipresent aspect of organisations- their culture. Culture may be broadly defined as "the way we do things here". It can be seen only through various factors like office layout, dress code, ways of communication, relationships between employees at different levels, language used, jargons, rituals, stories etc. It is based on the basic values, ideologies, assumptions and beliefs of the promoters and senior managers. It is like a glue that holds the organisation together. Based on his/her own beliefs and values, an individual may either fit in with the company's culture or feel uncomfortable working there.

2.2 Values and mission:

This takes us to the topic of mission, vision and values of an organisation. Values are what we believe in. Our personal values are shaped by values of our family, community and society. In an organisation, these are shaped by the values of promoters and senior managers. We need to learn and adjust to its values, beliefs and unwritten rules to work in harmony with our personal value system and that of the organisation. There are different layers of values like

• Individual- our own personal beliefs and values

• Group- working values and behaviour as followed by the sub-group of which you are a part

• Organisation- these are formed and shaped by the beliefs and values of the founders and senior managers

• Society- set of values shaped by shared beliefs based on historic and religious traditions prevalent in the larger society

2.3 Mission and Vision:

It is now almost universal today for every company to have a formally written mission and vision statement. Without going into semantics, we can treat both the words, vision and mission together. They are shaped by the values of the founders and basically outline the broad purpose beyond making just profits for which the organisation exists- the "why" of the organisation. This will lead us on to the aims and goals- or what the organisation hopes to achieve. The next level will be objectives and targets spelling out how we will reach there, giving specific time-bound milestones. This can be illustrated as follows:

• Why? – Mission and values – from broad purpose

- What? – Aims or goals

- How? – Objectives and targets

Formal mission statements help in spelling out the basic purposes of the organisation explicitly, communicating them to all the members and outside world and in decision making when major strategic decisions need to be taken so that they are in line with the mission of the company.

2.4 Ethics and morality:

Finally, as we saw earlier, when there is a conflict between your personal values and those based on demands of your job, you need to take your own decision on how far you are willing to compromise. Enlightened self-interest may dictate how far you are willing to toe the line. Thus, the question of ethics or morality is often personal. However, with increasing societal pressures, most of the organisations conform to generally accepted principles of ethical business norms and behaviour. They further encourage and reward their employees for ethical performance and punish unethical behaviour.

2.5 Models of organisational culture:

i. At the organisational levels, some models are used to categorise different culture types. One proposed by Prof. Charles Handy, an Irish legendary authority on organisational behaviour, lists four types of cultures as:

- Power culture, where power is centralised in one person or core, normally found when the company is run by founder/manager, strong-willed, believing in "command and control" approach

- Role culture, dominated by bureaucratic rules and regulations, as exemplified in government organisations

- Task culture, highly target and achievement oriented, thriving in high risk, target -oriented companies
- Person culture, where individuals in organisations enjoy power and status because of their specialised knowledge and skills, examples being educational institutions

ii.   Another model propounded by M/s. Deal and Kennedy, management authors, plots four types of culture on two axes of risk and feedback. The four quadrants of this two-by-two matrix represent:

- High risk, quick feedback - Macho culture
- High risk, slow feedback - Bet-your-company culture
- Low risk, quick feedback - Work hard, play hard culture
- Low risk, slow feedback – Process culture

Often, it is easy to fit in various companies under these different types in either model by observing their working even over a short period of time.

2.6   Changing organisational culture:

i.   As we saw earlier, cultural types also emerge at national, occupational and corporate levels. Changing organisational culture is very difficult. In today's business scenario with new challenges confronting them every day, companies are trying to change their cultures to meet the demands of businesses and environment. They try to do this through several measures like changing the reward system to encourage newer ways of working, role modelling, bringing in outsiders for senior positions, changing structure etc.

ii.   Organisations are channelling their cultural change effort in some of the following directions depending on corporate priorities:

- Technology orientation (IT and digitisation)
- Customer orientation (CRM- Customer Relationship Management)
- Quality orientation (TQM- Total Quality Management)
- Cost and process orientation (BPR- Business Process Reengineering)
- Human relations orientation (HRM- Human Resources Management)
- Environmental orientation (Green efforts)
- Ethics and social responsibility orientation (CSR- Corporate Social Responsibility)

However, these efforts often fail or take a long time to establish since existing cultures are deep-rooted and have been around for a long period especially in older organisations. Only a major threat to survival prompts and sustains these efforts, backed by active and continuous support by top management.

3. Organisation structure:

3.1 Structure:

One of the defining features of an organisation is its structure-formal and informal. The management differentiates various tasks to be performed and only through a structure, assigns them to individuals and departments with control and reporting systems in place. The same structure is used to integrate these efforts to achieve company's goals. We can define organisation structure in terms of following factors:

i. Span of control: This indicates how many sub-ordinates report to each manager which defines the scope of individual manager's job.

ii.   Hierarchy: Greater the number of layers, taller is the structure. This used to be the older way of structuring under "command and control" model of management with tight supervision at each level. However, with growing complexity, modern organisations have a flatter structure with fewer levels of reporting, offering greater flexibility and freedom to sub-ordinates.

iii. Centralisation: In highly centralised organisations, decision making rests at the very top. Again, this was the earlier style when businesses were simple, small and were totally run by entrepreneur-managers, who took all the decisions. Today decision making is often de-centralised and widely distributed at all levels.

iv.   Specialisation: Breaking tasks into finer details and assigning them to individuals, teams and departments is called specialisation. This is especially true in the case of jobs requiring specialised knowledge and skills. Specialisation gives several advantages in executing highly specialised jobs in high tech companies. But it often leads to "silos" mentality among individuals and teams, lack of awareness of company's overall goals and also conflicts and ego clashes among people and departments. Achieving right degree of specialisation will ensure attention to specialised jobs while also ensuring integration of these through general management team.

v.   Unity and chain of command: These are borrowed from the structure of armed forces where discipline and clarity are of utmost importance. Also, in organisations where the priority tasks are clear and the top leader and his/her team have all the required information and knowledge to make complex decisions and at times of crisis, unity of command is essential to ensure speedy implementation.

However, in modern complex business organisations where specialists and generalists have to work together, this may not always be the best principle. Down the line, people may have to report to and take directions from two or more persons. For example, in high tech companies, a field sales executive will have to take directions from a functional manager like sales or marketing manager and also a product specialist manager with special technical knowledge on the product/service. This is true with more and more specialisation in multi-product organisations.

vi.   Communication process: The communication process is an integral part of an organisation where people have come together to fulfil their objectives as well as that of the organisation. It helps in several core functions like

- Communicating the roles and responsibilities, targets, achievements etc to individuals, groups and departments and give effective feedback

- Planning, co-ordinating and controlling operations

- Communicating overall performance of the company, its strategies and plan of action

- Presenting company's activities and results achieved to all stakeholders and outside world

Successful communication is a two-way process- listening as well as talking or informing. Hence, creating and maintaining an open and supportive communication climate is essential in modern business organisations rather than closed one-way communication which is still prevalent in many companies with underlying "command and control" assumptions.

Apart from providing a framework for defining individual roles and responsibilities, a well-defined organisation structure creates an identity for the organisation and provides for continuity and change. The communication aspect of the structure enables participation of all employees in the achievement of its overall goals.

However, by putting people in neatly- defined albeit constrictive boxes, a too rigid a structure will stifle creativity and is an impediment in implementing right decisions in times of crisis, especially when there is a disconnect between the real problem and the top management's understanding of it.

3.2 Types of organisational structures:

Companies may be organised in many ways. Some popular models are as follows:

i.   Functional: Here, the company is structured along functional lines like Manufacturing, Marketing, Finance, Human Resources Management (HRM) etc, all the functional heads reporting to General Management people. The number of departments depends on the degree of specialisation needed and complexities. As we had seen earlier, while this is necessary since each functional area requires different skills and knowledge and to ensure special attention to each, this will become dysfunctional when people in each functional area start thinking of themselves as a separate group and work for maximising the output of their own functions only, at the expense of overall company goals.

ii. Products or Services: Companies with several product lines each requiring high technical inputs and also serving different markets and customers, are structured along specific product/ service lines, all reporting to the senior management. Here again, the pitfall to be avoided is the "silos" mentality.

iii. Geographical: In situations where the company operates in various regions and countries with different customer profile, business laws and practices and stages of development, it is organised along geographical lines, country-wise and/or region-wise.

iv. Matrix structure: As we discussed earlier, in companies which deal with high tech products or operate in special markets where there is a need to provide direct guidelines to line people below by a senior technical person, a matrix structure is recommended. There is a dual reporting relationship here. Under this structure, a line manager may be reporting to Corporate Head of a functional area as well as to a Product Head or a Country Head.

v. In corporations which have multiple products and operate in multiple regions within a country, the corporation is structured along independent products or markets called Strategic Business Units (SBUs). Each SBU becomes an independent profit centre responsible for profits from these products, services or regions with a central corporate head office setting the overall direction.

vi. Corporations which operate in several countries, are structured depending on where the decisions are made. In Multi-National Corporations (MNCs), these are at country levels. In international organisations, they follow a matrix structure. In global organisations, the strategic decision-making process is primarily centralised.

Nowadays these differences are often blurred, and companies adopt mixed/hybrid structures depending on the factors given below.

3 Factors influencing choice of structure:

Following factors influence the choice of organisational structure:

i. Size in terms of number of people, product lines, degree of specialisation in terms of products/ markets

ii. Technology

iii. Strategy

iv. Culture

v. Need for change

4. Organisations as systems:

We will now move on to look at the idea of organisations as systems. This helps us in understanding many aspects of organisation.

4.1 What is a system?

A system has certain basic characteristics as follows:

i. A system is a collection of sub-systems or parts that are integrated to achieve an overall goal. We have seen that an organisation is a system of people coming together to achieve certain goals- a human system.

ii. Systems and sub-systems have certain inputs and processes to convert these inputs to desired outputs There is close interaction between sub-systems and in the case of an organisation, various sub-systems like Production, Marketing etc interact.

iii. If one or more sub-systems or parts of a system are removed, then the nature of system undergoes change We can see that in an organisation where all activitie were carried out in-house, if one function is taken out an outsourced, the organisation changes.

4.2 Some Systems principles:

i. The overall behaviour or working of a system is dependent on the entire structure and not just a sum of its parts. Th output of the system is greater than sum of its parts. Hence the idea of synergy in organisations.

ii. The system can be big or small depending on the number of sub-systems. There is no limit to its size. For example, government is a huge system with innumerable sub-systems.

iii. Since systems exist in an external environment, they need to achieve balance with their environment. In the case of organisations, they need to satisfy customer needs and fulfil expectations of other stakeholders.

iv. When a system ignores this principle by not interacting with the external environment, it will not last long. Organisations too can survive and grow only when they interact and get inputs/feedback from the external environment on a continuing basis.

4.3 Organisation as an open system:

As we just saw, an organisation is a system with certain inputs, conversion processes and outputs and operates in an external environment as an open system.

i. The inputs are in terms of finance, people, technology, plant and machinery, data and information etc. The conversion process consists of Purchase, Production and Marketing activities, R & D, Planning and Control activities etc. The outputs include products and services and scrap or wastage. Some organisations turn out ideas and reports as in the case of consulting firms and auditing firms.

ii.   Traditionally, most of the conversion activities were being carried out within the organisation. However, since it is operating as an open system in an environment, it has the option of getting some of the activities done by other systems in the economy. With more and more specialisations and technological advancements, modern organisations retain core activities within their system and outsource other activities from outside. For example, many companies outsource peripheral activities like security, catering etc from other entities who are specialists in these which are their core activities and main business. Today with more and more specialisations, companies even outsource their R & D, Accounting etc. In fact, the phenomenal growth of Indian IT industry is entirely attributable to this global trend. "Make or Buy" is the watchword and several factors need to be considered in taking suitable decisions on what activities are to be carried out in-house and what should be outsourced or bought from outside.

4.4   Make in-house or outsource:

Following are the advantages of making in house:

- Companies will have total control especially on quality

- This is more dependable than relying on outsourcing

- Company's experience and expertise in making it in-house are also a major advantage

- Resource allocation becomes more flexible depending on the need to divert resources from one activity to another

The disadvantages are:

- Since these are not core activities, there are limits to achieving economies of scale
- Costs will be higher in most cases because of greater overhead costs compared to smaller organisations
- Since these will only be peripheral activities, company may not be keeping track of latest technological developments in these areas

Outsourcing advantages:

- Lower costs of manufacturing since suppliers will be able to take advantage of economies of scale and lower overheads due to lower manpower, machines and inventory costs to be allotted to the company's products alone
- It releases time of managers to concentrate on the firm's core activities

Outsourcing disadvantages:

- Loss of control, especially on quality and price
- Risks of disruption in supplies
- Loss of in-house expertise and dependence on supplier for newer technologies

4.5 Transaction costs:

When a firm decides to outsource some of its activities, it needs to consider additional transaction costs that will be involved. These include costs that will be incurred in finalising, monitoring, controlling and managing the transactions. This is apart from comparison of other costs/benefits as discussed earlier.

Transaction cost theory was propounded and developed by Prof. Williamson, an American economist. Transaction costs are a major determinant in outsourcing decisions.

5. Business processes:

i. Business processes: We will now look at business processes which form a part each firm's method of operations. Processes define how we do things here and can be illustrated as follows:

- Why are we doing this? – Mission and Vision

- What do we want to achieve? – Objectives

- How are we going to do? – Processes

ii. Defining a business process: A business process consists of a set of activities giving the sequence in which they are done. It defines the inputs and outputs at each stage to produce a specific result. They consist of primary processes that ultimately result in the final product/ service received by the customer. Support processes are services that aid in turning out the end product/service, hence not seen in the final offering.

iii. Organisations and their leaders often work with two dominant orientations where tasks and processes are involved:

- Task orientation: Here the main concentration is on the tasks to be done with little regard for how the tasks are done. "Do somehow" is the culture or mantra here, often the underlying assumption in many for-profit organisations.

- Process orientation: "How to do" is the predominant disposition here with scant attention to tasks and results. Government and business offer several examples for this orientation. As they say, doting the "I" s and crossing the "t" s are paramount here and the total message gets lost in the process.

To be successful, organisations should develop high task and high process orientations simultaneously. This is easily said than done and the top leader and his team need to lead by example here. This leads to higher moral and ethical behaviour of the firms.

6.   Business strategy:

Business strategy is a vast subject in itself and has been the primary focus of CEOs of all major corporations and business thinkers all over the world. I do not think I can do full justice to this subject matter even briefly in this short booklet, more so just as a part of it.

However, I feel this topic fits perfectly in this booklet since business strategy is all about running an organisation to achieve its objectives. Strategy making rests with the very top but involves everyone in its execution, hence this fit in this booklet on managing in organisations. Also, subsequent booklets will cover function-wise concepts and practices in business management, and it stands to reason that they flow out of the company's overall business strategy.

5.1   Holistic and long-term:

It is often said that what distinguishes a winner from a loser, a successful firm from a demised, losing or "also ran" firm, is its business strategy. Until recent times, when the external environment was stable and reasonably predictable, business strategy was defined by two terms- holistic and long-term. In modern turbulent business environment, this definition is to be modified to the extent that strategy may have to be reviewed continuously and specific aspects need to be modified based on this monitoring, rather than the holistic, long-term strategy of the firm. However, the strategy makers have to ensure that these course corrections are in line with the long-term mission of the company. It is just that strategy making has become more fragmented and some aspects of strategy have a short-term orientation. This is primarily due to constantly evolving technological advances and complex external environment, posing both challenges to the present strategy and at the same time, offering new opportunities.

We need to understand and differentiate tactical decisions from strategic ones. In general, we can say that all short-term decisions to adjust our activities to specific short-term events and/or combat competition come under tactical moves. Short-term sales promotional offers, temporary addition to manpower, buying materials one time from a new source etc are all tactical decisions. However, we should ensure that these tactical decisions do not go contrary to the strategic direction the company plans to move which is holistic and long term.

In this section, we will outline a basic approach to strategy, the strategy process and recent developments that are shaping strategies of companies.

6.2   The basic approach:

Basically, a firm's business strategy is an exercise in developing and matching the goals, values, structures, systems, resources and capabilities of the firm with the opportunities available in the industry and business environment. Following are the defining characteristics of successful business strategies:

- A thorough understanding of the industry and general business environment

- An objective and realistic assessment of company's resources

- A well-developed long-term vision and consistent objectives

- A robust business strategy matching the resources of the company with the opportunities available to reach its objectives on a dynamic basis

- Effective implementation

A basic tenet of business is that strategy is a matter of choice. Companies examine several factors and alternatives available to arrive at their long-term business strategies. Based on their analysis, choices need to be made on the following:

i. What is the nature, domain and scope of our business? What is our long-term vision? This is to say that we need to choose what industry we want to be in, what we want to achieve, at what scale and to what extent we are looking at the scope or boundaries of our activities.

ii. These are based on our study of larger business environment and specific industry environment.

iii. Once we have broadly made this choice, we need to plan and acquire resources needed and allocate them among various activities.

iv. We need to arrive at what capabilities we need to build to succeed in the industry. This involves study of key success factors.

v. Thus we have to match our resources and capabilities with the challenges and opportunities in the business and industry environments.

vi. We also need to create and manage networks of relation-ships with all our stakeholders.

vii.   We have to keep evaluating success of our activities with suitable measures and reviewing our strategic approach on a dynamic basis.

All these aspects of the basic approach to strategy are discussed in detail in the following sections.

6.3   Some basic thoughts on strategy:

i.   In large corporations, strategies are developed at different levels like

- Internal business units called Strategic Business Units (SBUs)
- Total business strategy pertaining to specific business/industry
- Corporate strategy where the corporation operates in multiple businesses – products and markets

ii.   In a larger sense, the role of strategy includes the following:

- It defines the targets or objectives and milestones
- It acts as a support for decision making in complex situations, to align decisions with strategy
- Strategy is used to design and develop the company's mission statement which serves as the means of communication within and outside the company/corporation

iii.   Often, due to various external and internal factors, while the company may have a clearly defined strategy, implemented strategy turns out to be different. The emerging strategy may turn out be further different.

On top of this, in many instances while the business environment may be changing rapidly, companies make only incremental changes due to complacency based on their past successful record. One of the famous quotes from Prof. Richard Pascale, leading management professor and consultant, goes like this: "Nothing succeeds success like failure".

Over a period of time, the gap between the strategy required and actually achieved, grows very wide and there will be a need for the companies to undergo rapid business transformation. If they do not take suitable decisive actions and transform themselves at these critical inflection points, they further degenerate and will ultimately die. The business world is littered with several companies that met with their demise due to their hubris.

6.4 The strategy development process:

We will discuss a three-stage model of strategy development process proposed by Prof. Johnson and Scholes, eminent management thinkers. The three overlapping stages are:

i.   Strategic analysis: This phase consists of analysing the larger business and industry environment and company's resources and strategic capabilities in terms of its strengths and weaknesses.

ii. Strategic choice: At this stage, companies look at all stakeholders and their expectations, fix mission and objectives, identify and evaluate the options available and select the most appropriate strategy to attain their goals and objectives.

iii. Strategy implementation: Finally, companies plan and allocate resources to various activities to be carried out, create necessary organisation structure for implementation and manage the outcomes in the emergent strategy including the company's culture as it emerges over a period of time.

We will now look at steps involved in each of these stages.

7.   Strategic analysis:

7.1   Approaches:

Basically, there are two schools of thought on where to start your strategic analysis and with different emphasis. The first approach based on Prof. Michael Porter's theory of competitive advantage, places emphasis on the analysis of overall business environment and industry environment first. The second one called resource-based approach to strategy as propagated by Profs. Hamel and Prahalad and others, starts with an analysis of company's resources and capabilities. This approach states that a company may have several resources in the form of money, manpower, plant and machinery, technology, patents, information, relationships etc. While resources by themselves will not produce results, a combination of resources brought together in an optimal mix for the tasks on hand, produces the results expected. This is called capability and defined as core competence by them. Thus, while resources form the basis of firm's capabilities, capabilities alone give it competitive advantage. This means that by building up its capabilities, the company is able to do better than competition in delivering value to its customers and thereby achieve desired results.

In the ultimate analysis, both lead to matching resources and capabilities with the opportunities available in the larger business and specific industry environments. We will be looking at both of them together when we talk of strategic analysis.

7.2   Developing a mission:

We will start with the steps to be taken to arrive at the mission of the company.

i. Purpose: Arrive at and finalise the larger purpose of the company, apart from making profits.

ii. Values: These are what the promoters believe in and guide the company's activities.

iii. Policies and Standards of behaviour: Arising out of these, the company formulates its policies and sets standards of behaviour that define its value system and its distinctive competence.

iv. The final step will be to formulate the company's strategy. It spells out the company's competitive stance and distinctive competences through which it will achieve its competitive advantage.

7.3 Multiple stakeholders and multiple expectations:

A company cannot declare that profit alone is the main purpose of its business. There are multiple stakeholders who are interested in profitable operations of the company, but with multiple primary expectations as given below:

Stakeholders	Primary expectations
i. Owners or shareholders	Financial return
ii. Employees	Pay
iii. Customers	Value for money
iv. Creditors who lend money	Creditworthiness
v. Suppliers who supply raw materials, components, services etc.	Timely payments, regular orders
vi. Government	Job creation, Compliance with laws of the country
vii. Community	Jobs, safety, environment

To achieve its objectives on a long -term basis, the company has to take into consideration all their expectations. Balancing these expectations is no mean task and is probably the most challenging job of top management.

Taking this point further, in today's competitive business environment, CEOs and senior managers are driven to direct their company's strategy towards maximising short-term profits, or quarter-to-quarter earnings. While this may satisfy the shareholders or the stock market in the short term, even they want their investments to grow in the long run. Short-termism is of interest only to speculative traders in the stock market, looking for a kill in the short run. All stakeholders too expect the firm to grow on a strong footing in the long run. This should be the long term, holistic purpose of strategy and act as the guiding principle. Notwithstanding this self-evident truth, CEOs often concentrate on quarter-to-quarter results since their compensation is based on these short-term results.

7.4 External environment analysis:

i. While the industry environment consists of customers, competitors, suppliers and distribution channel members, the larger business environment consists of:

- National and global, economic and politica environments
- Natural environment which is decaying day-by da and is the concern of everyone today
- Market environment consisting of customer profile and choices, demographics, emerging trends etc.
- Social environment which covers societal value structures, norms and behaviour

- Technological environment concerning both specific industry-related and other newer technologies in various fields like Manufacturing, IT, Logistics etc.

ii. We can thus think of three circles of environment:

- Internal environment consisting of your own organisation's internal factors that you can control

- Near industry environment consisting of suppliers, customers, even competitors etc, all of whom you can influence to an extent

- Far environment, the larger environment where you can only respond to developments either reactively or proactively

iii. Larger external environment: All factors mentioned above, are designated by the acronym STEEP:

S – Sociological

T – Technological

E – Economic

E – Environmental

P – Political

We list below the various factors in each of them which need to be studied and understood.

- Sociological: Demographic profiles like age, sex, education, occupation, urban and rural, gender roles etc, structure of families like nuclear, joint, extended etc, religious and cultural traditions and practices, consumption and shopping priorities, patterns etc.

- Technological: General current technological practices and emerging trends, impact of new technologies and industries, resultant job obsolescence and emerging new skill requirements

- Economic: When we look at the larger economic scenario in the country, some of the major factors to be considered are:

  a) Rate of economic growth: How is the economy growing, measured by GDP? Which sectors, which markets?

  b) Inflation rate: This will indicate the movement in prices to see whether they are in line with growth

  c) Interest rates: Related to inflation, you can find out what the real returns are.

  d) Rate of unemployment and availability of workforce with required skills

  e) Exchange rate of national currency

  f) Cost of industry inputs like power etc

  g) State of infrastructure

  Taken together, they represent the state of the economy.

- Environmental: Pollution levels, Level of deforestation, changes in climatic conditions, environmental regulations etc

- Political:

  a) Stability status of central and state governments, stated policies of different political parties and their leaders

  b) Policies and legislations on general areas like health, safety, reservations etc

  c) Taxation and trade policies on property, income, sales, customs etc

d)   Corporate governance policies and laws like statutory reports on income, ownership etc, auditing requirements, Corporate Social Responsibility (CSR) etc

e)   Trade blocks and trade agreements etc

7.5   Industry analysis:

As we saw just now, the industry environment in which a company operates comprises of customers, competitors, suppliers, distribution channel partners (supply chain) etc. To look at the industry environment as a whole, companies start with a framework developed by Prof. Michael Porter, called the Five Forces framework.

For a new company to decide whether to invest in a particular industry or for an existing firm in an industry to study the state of the industry, the basic criterion to assess is called the industry's attractiveness, which is also reflected by industry rivalry within it. Making this as the central force, Michael Porter's model lists four other factors which affect the industry rivalry. Taken together, a detailed analysis of the following five forces gives a picture of the present state of industry:

- Industry rivalry
- Threat of substitutes
- Threat of entry
- Buyer power
- Supplier power

We will now discuss factors to be considered under each one of them.

i.   Industry rivalry: Following factors are analysed here:

a) Age of the industry: is it a mature or sunrise industry judged by present and future growth potential

b) Status of competition: How many competitors, their size, share and spread like small, medium or large companies and their perceived strengths, weaknesses, resources and capabilities, strategies etc and how they will respond to our strategy

c) Range of products/services offered by the industry- how are they differentiated from one another and how customers view them

d) What other industries are connected to this industry and their profiles

e) Capacity utilisation in the industry in what segments

f) Prevailing cost conditions: what are the cost drivers and who controls them

g) Exit barriers: How difficult it is to get out of the industry in terms of investments made, technology obsolescence, manpower restrictions, government regulations etc

h) Entry barriers: How difficult to enter this industry in terms of specialised technology, manpower, financial outlay, location, capabilities to build etc.

Industry rivalry is further influenced by the following forces as mentioned above.

ii. Threat of substitutes: What are the substitute products/ services available that can replace industry's offerings – their relative prices, performance and customer perceptions and preferences

iii. Threat of entry: Are the entry barriers mentioned above surmountable? Other factors to study include economies of scale to be achieved to be viable, capital required, cost advantages of existing players, emergence of new products and new technologies, legal protections etc. Threat of new entrants is high, if all these challenges are surmountable without great difficulty.

iv. Buyer power: How differentiated the products and services offered by this industry are, buyers' dependence on them, buyers'/buyer industries' profiles and their price sensitivity

v. Supplier power: Bargaining power of suppliers of raw materials, components etc relative to that of industry players. For example, if you are looking at an industry converting steel to end products, suppliers of steel will have greater power due to their size, diverse customer base etc.

If our analysis of above forces reveals that industry rivalry is high, threat of substitutes is imminent, threat of entry is high, buyer power and supplier power are also high, then that industry may not be attractive for newcomers. But for an existing firm, this analysis will reveal the areas to concentrate and the direction to go while formulating its strategy. However, there are examples of companies which entered even such "unattractive" industries and succeeded by opening new markets and redefining the industry itself, through their clever and unorthodox strategies. We shall see more on this later in this section.

Further, two caveats are in order here. The first one is that the five forces analysis often tends to be indicative of the status of the industry as on today. Even industry insiders may not have all relevant information to make a fully informed assessment of the future prospects. Secondly, in today's dynamic business environment, newer and emerging technologies have made the industry boundaries hazy as they run across and link several industries into one. Also, applications of these technologies completely transform the competitive scenarios in the industry.

However, the five forces framework still remains a major tool in strategy analysis.

7.6 Key success factors:

In a competitive situation, as a general rule we can say that there are two requirements for a firm to succeed. First, it should have some specific advantage over competitors. Secondly, the company's products should be the preferred one in the "buy" basket of customers, at a price which covers the costs and margins of the company. The firm can achieve these by analysing competition on one hand and customers and markets on the other.

This analysis should lead the firm to arrive at how to gain advantage over competitors and also what factors influence customers' choice. Thus, the factors required to succeed in a competitive industry called the key success factors, are derived from this twin analysis of customers and competition. We had earlier seen what factors are considered in our industry and competition analysis under the Five Forces Framework and we now outline below steps involved in arriving at customer choice through an analysis of customer segments.

7.7 Analysis of customer segments:

We saw earlier that a company cannot be everything to every body. Hence it is imperative for the company to do a customer segment analysis consisting of following steps:

- Define the variables that distinguish segments like customer demographic profiles, literacy rates, urban/rural household expenditure levels etc

- Find out the attractiveness of each segment in terms of share of each segment of the total market, profits that ca be generated, ease of servicing and willingness to pay a price that will cover our costs and margins

- Similarly, industrial products markets are also analysed based on customer industry requirements in terms of products, performance and service, their end-customer requirements, size, location, technology used etc
- Finally, arrive at the key success factors to service these segments

This exercise is primarily part of Marketing team's responsibilities, and we will be discussing customer segment analysis in greater detail in the booklet on Marketing Management.

7.8 Strategic space analysis:

This is a key factor in the formulation of company's strategy. Here we deal with the idea of finalising a strategic space in a highly competitive industry, which is hitherto not explored, and which offers potential.

i. With the development of highly sophisticated marketing research tools and techniques like conjoint analysis etc, companies are in a position to understand the preferences of customers in various segments more accurately. Based on these insights, companies are able to develop and offer new product concepts and positioning strategies which are altogether different from existing products and services in an already over-crowded market/industry. This concept of strategic space positioning in uncharted waters, developed by Profs. W. Chan Kim and Renee Mauborgne is aptly called the "blue ocean strategy" as against red ocean where existing companies, fiercely compete with each other with marginally differentiated offerings.

This they can do by developing "value curves" for each segment. Value curves represent what features and benefits the customers in that particular segment would be willing to pay for and what they would be willing to give up instead. Thus, for each segment, you can incur more "good costs" to incorporate these preferred features and benefits and reduce or eliminate "bad costs" on those that customer would give up. You can also arrive at what customers would pay for this offering. One example of a company that had used conjoint analysis with other marketing research tools is Marriot group of hotels in the USA. When they found that the market for their full-range, high-end chain of hotels, located in busy areas, was nearing saturation levels, they carried out extensive market research to come out with a new hotel concept. The result was the Courtyard by Marriot chain of hotels which was aimed at business and middle level security-conscious travellers whose needs were not served in the industry. They built in features and attributes that matched with their requirements. These travellers placed more emphasis on security, bed and bath comfort and a built-in office table and were willing to settle down for self-check-in, limited range restaurants and not city-central locations for a given price. Ginger group of hotels from Tata's is also based on similar approach.

ii. Another strategic choice arising out of this strategic space analysis, is called "reverse positioning" and allied new positioning strategies. Here, the companies are able to create new strategic space by moving away from estab-lished segments and creating a new segment/segments. An example of this is the positioning of IKEA, the European furniture manufacturer. They succeeded in the American furniture market by borrowing features of the extreme ends of the market. One is the high-end, multi design, full range, high inventory, expensive chain furniture shops offering advice from specialists on furniture selection. The other end consists of minimum quality, minimum range, minimum cost, low-end single shops. IKEA created a new segment of cost-conscious segment of young customers, making shopping experience as the main attraction. The company offered minimum range in each type of furniture, standard quality acceptable at the price offered, self-assembly and self-transportable furniture in completely knocked-down condition. Thus, they eliminated all "bad costs" for this segment and added on "good costs" to be incurred to give that unique shopping experience. By sourcing components from all over the world at the lowest costs, the company's total costs were brought down. Thus, they created a new value curve.

Similarly, Starbucks made coffee drinking very popular in the USA where it was not a major market. At one end, there were high speciality single stores offering exotic flavours of coffee at very high prices. And there were many small, lowly-differentiated, low-cost stores at the other end, offering minimal coffee experience. Starbucks came in with two distinct value propositions – one, a big range of speciality coffees to suit well-to-do individual customer's tastes and two, personalised attention to individual customers. Their chain of coffee shops in multiple locations were tastefully decorated providing private space for customers. They were seen as "a third place, apart from home and office". Thus, coffee drinking in Starbucks was seen as a personal indulgence, since they charged the highest prices, a new position for a new segment.

Through gaining insight into preferences of hitherto unknown and unserved market segments, these companies created an altogether new strategic space and dominated the markets as leaders.

7.9 Resource-based approach to strategy:

We will now move on to see how we can match the resources and capabilities of the firm with the opportunities available in the larger business and industry environment. First, let us look at the relationship between our resources and capabilities, key success factors to succeed in the industry and strategy required that will give us the necessary competitive advantage.

i.   As we had seen earlier, companies have/acquire certain resources which can be grouped as under:

   •   Tangible: Financial and physical like plant & machinery etc

   •   Intangible: Ownership of patented technologies, company image, company's culture, relationships etc

   •   Human: Specialised skills and knowledge of key employees, managerial abilities, motivation of employees etc

      By combining these resources and bringing them together, they build and establish organisation's capabilities to excel in certain tasks.

ii. We now look at the key success factors that dictate success in the industry and match our capabilities to these key success factors through our strategy, to arrive at our competitive advantage. A few points are worth noting here:

   •   We should leverage our resources or make maximum use of our resources by concentrating them on our key tasks and goals, since resources are scarce. At the same time, we will do well by remembering that just increasing the efficiency is not the answer. While we should leverage our resources for maximum competitive advantage, we should also provide for some "slack" resources so that they can be put to use at very short notice ahead of competition when an opportunity or challenge arises. An example would be investments in R & D whereby when a new technology emerges and customer requirements and expectations change rapidly, we can be prepared.

• Mere fit is not enough. We need to stretch our resources and capabilities for continuous improvement, to achieve dynamic fit with our ambitions and aspirations. This is to say that we should aim for achievement of something greater than just what the external environment offers now.

• We should move from just single task capability to specialised, activities-based and cross-functional capabilities to achieve maximum competitive advantage.

In this regard, we can look at a new way of classifying a firm's capabilities as processes. A strategic management author has classified a firm's capabilities into:

* Outside-in processes where the emphasis is on external activities - example: Marketing research; Trade relations

* Inside-out processes that take place primarily within the organisation -example: R & D; Cost Management

* Spanning processes that run through the firm and link internal and external activities– Customer order fulfilment; Customer service

- Some of the capabilities mentioned above, may reside informally within certain people and groups. By putting in place systems and processes formally, these capabilities become regular processes to be followed and no more dependent on individuals and groups. This forms part of Knowledge Management initiatives of the company.

- Benchmarking is a tool employed by companies to set higher standards for their performance in specific areas and capability building by comparing them with market leaders in that area either in their own industry or in any other industry and ramp up those capabilities to match the performance of bench-marked companies. It could be with regard to quality, delivery time, cost etc.

iii.   Defining competitive advantage: We can say that a company has competitive advantage over another one in the same industry supplying to the same customer segment when it earns a higher rate of return at present or in a position to do so in the future.

We know that a company's resources and capabilities give it the competitive advantage and we can assess their profit earning potential based on the following criteria:

- Are they scarce and are they relevant to our industry They will lose their edge if they are available in plent and if they are not relevant to our industry.

- Can the competitive advantage be sustained ove long term- how durable they are?

- To what extent they can be replicated or transferred

- To what extent the company can protect the without hurting its capacity to realise its maximu market potential? This depends on to what extent v can protect them through copyright etc, our relative bargaining power with customers and proprietorship of resources.

By building appropriate resources and capabilities based on above analysis, a company can gain superior competitive advantage over other competitors in the industry.

v. Bringing all this together, we can summarise resource-based approach to strategy analysis as follows:

- Build resources and capabilities that will give the best competitive advantage in our industry

- Develop our business strategy based on matching these to key success factors

- Leverage and stretch our resources for maximum benefit

- Continuously evaluate and build up our resources and capabilities to sustain our competitive advantage

B. Strategy choice:

. Sources of competitive advantage: We can say that the company can pursue several options to gain competitive advantage which can emerge from either external sources of change or internal sources of change.

i. The external sources include:

- Technology changes

- Changing customer needs and choices

- Pricing changes

Companies may add resources required to cope with these changes but exploiting the opportunities arising out of

them depend on the firm's ability to forecast and reac
faster to these changes.

iii.   Internal sources: These basically consist of its creative anc
innovative abilities through R & D efforts and foresight o
management.

9.   Generic strategies:

Prof. Michael Porter postulated that there are two major route:
to obtain competitive advantage as follows:

*   Cost advantage whereby the firm is able to offer simila
    product to its customers at a lower cost

*   Differentiation advantage wherein the firm is able tc
    realise greater price or price premium by offering a
    differentiated product.

Using this approach, He further developed a two-by-two matri:
based on specific focus on the markets served by the firm
resulting in four generic strategies as given below:

*   Broad coverage:
    a)   Cost leadership on the entire range of customers anc
          markets
    b)   Broad differentiation on the entire range

*   Narrow focus:
    a)   Cost focus on selected customers, markets anc
          products
    b)   Differentiation focus on selected markets anc
          products

By and large, this model has been behind the thinking of strategies of many companies.

10. Cost advantage:

Companies strive to achieve cost advantage by following ways:

- Economies of scale which will bring down input costs
- Faster learning curve leading to higher capacity utilisation at the earliest
- Product design through creative thinking
- Production techniques through organisational efficiencies

10.1 Concept of value chain:

i. Prof. Porter has further developed a framework called "value chain" that helps companies analyse their costs and bring them down to have cost advantage over their competitors. The value chain analysis consists of first dividing the activities of the firm into primary and secondary activities.

ii. Primary activities consist of:

- In-bound logistics: Receiving, storing and handling materials
- Operations: Manufacturing, assembly, packaging
- Outbound logistics: Storing finished goods, distributing, shipping
- Marketing and sales: Personal selling, advertising, sales promotions
- Sales service: Installation, repair and maintenance, supply of spare parts

iii. The support activities include:

- Firm's infrastructure: General management, planning, finance, plant maintenance etc
- Human resources management: Recruitment, training, development
- Technology development: R& D for development of new products and processes
- Procurement: Purchase of raw materials, components etc

Together, these activities turn out products/services, reach them to customers and also offer them after-sales services.

These broad range of activities are further dived into sub-activities and each one of them is costed considering its importance and relevance to total costs and identifying drivers that lead to these costs.

iv. To obtain cost advantage, these costs are then compared with those of market leaders chosen for benchmarking and opportunities for reducing them are located and implemented.

v. When companies have lost their way and struggle for survival, this cost reduction exercise will include extreme steps like

- Plant closures and laying off of people to reduce manpower costs
- Outsourcing components and activities
- Reducing management staff strength by eliminating layers, combining job responsibilities etc

All these are part of what is called Business Process Reengineering (BPR).

It is a fact that over a period of time, if they do not watch out, companies put on "fat or layers" and become inefficient. They lose touch with external environment and become complacent with their past achievements, hoping that they can somehow survive by running "business as usual". There comes a critical point at which a major surgery as mentioned above, will be required.

However, many companies take up this challenge and opportunity to reinvent themselves by changing themselves through BPR techniques. This concept was first developed by Prof. Michael Hammer in early 1990s and soon had a lot of followers to become a much used and abused concept and practice in many companies. An unwanted side effect of this was that companies reverted back to "command and control" model of management and started cutting jobs indiscriminately.

11. Differentiation advantage:

i. Many leading organisations seem to opt for this strategy by building up several advantages over competitors to differentiate themselves from the "pack". They arrive at their differentiation strategy from an analysis of two sides-demand and supply.

ii. On the demand side, they look at it from product and customer angles that help them in formulating their differentiation approach. They analyse what customer needs the product satisfies and what attributes customer looks in for when choosing a product. They also look at the demographic profiles of the customers, what motivates them to buy and what price premium the customers are willing to pay for certain attributes over others.

Armed with this data, companies select their target customer segments, product positioning for these segments by building in the preferred features and attributes that will enhance customer value and reducing those that do not add value. These form the basis of their differentiation strategy.

iii. On the supply side, they look at to what extent and where they can build in or enhance these attributes by analysing the entire value chain.

iv. In effect, first they develop value curves for various customer segments as we had seen earlier and second, a value chain for the company's offerings and ensure that these two are matched to offer unique customer experience, at a price acceptable to them as well as meet with the profit objectives of the company.

v. Extensions of this differentiation strategy are the special ones we saw earlier- blue ocean strategy, reverse positioning etc. These help the company chart out a new course in terms of products and markets in an over-crowded industry or create a new market which is untapped by competition.

12. Strategy implementation:

i. We saw earlier that strategy means holistic and long-term. One may wonder how long-term thinking is possible in a dynamic business world. Technology seems to be changing the way we do things almost every day. The answer may be that while we need to adjust our short-term activities, tactics and even goals, we need to be guided by our broad long-term mission in our overall approach. It is like taking a diversion or detour when there is a roadblock, to reach our final destination. We should also know at what stage of evolution our industry is in. Just like all living organisms including human beings, industries also go through the life cycle of birth, growth, maturity and decline. Strategy adjustments are necessary at each stage of the cycle.

ii. What is critical is that companies should know when they are nearing the top of the maturity phase and implement necessary break-away strategies that will once again put them on growth path instead of stagnation and decline. The new approaches to strategy making like the blue ocean strategy and reverse positioning are examples of this. However, this is easily said than done since companies become complacent, resting on their laurels based on past successes. They continue to march on trodden path when the external environment has changed dramatically. That is why top management and senior managers of companies should be scanning the environment continuously and keep abreast of developments in larger as well as industry environments. They should develop their skills in locating the "weak signals" which are often buried in the din and noise of other developments that send out "strong signals" which can be picked up easily by any observer. All companies tend to respond to these strong signals uniformly, given our "herd mentality".

iii. There are also totally unexpected, one of a kind, rarest of rare instances that turn the whole world upside down. Prof. Nassim Nicholas Taleb called these the "black swan" events in his book of the same title. As I am writing this booklet during the months of March and April 2020, we are in the midst of one such "black swan" instance of the uncontrollable "Corona virus" or "COVID-19" spreading all over the world. Nobody has ever predicted such an event or are we near any tangible solution yet, to fight this demon. However, we can only minimise our risks of exposure to such a catastrophic event by relying on humanity's past experiences and put forth our best efforts to contain and conquer the virus through scientific research and development.

13. How industries evolve and reach maturity stage:

Major factors that lead to industries reaching the maturity stage can be listed as follows:

i.   Technology becomes available to all manufacturers in the industry.

ii.   Customers have gained a lot of experience in using the product and are fully knowledgeable about its costs, prices, attributes, preferences etc.

iii. Market demand for the product slows down at this saturation point and there is evidence of excess capacity in the industry.

As illustrated by Prof. Robert M. Grant in his book, "Contemporary Strategy Analysis" (listed under primary reference books) these lead to the following:

i.   Products become more or less standardised with hardly any differentiation.

ii.   Customers become more price-conscious and are no willing to pay price premiums.

iii. Management concentration turns to production efficiency (lower costs) with less emphasis on R & D.

iv.   Where the labour content is high, parts of manufacturing activities are sub-contracted or production facilities are shifted to countries where labour costs are low.

v.   Firms seek to create more and more differentiation. These measures do not appeal to customers and also do no fetch any price premiums to enable the companies to absorb additional costs. Price war intensifies in the industry.

vi.   Distribution channels become powerful because of their proximity to customers, chipping away firm's margins o start marketing products under their own brands resulting in further competition.

When these happen, the markets have truly matured and may be on the way to decline.

14. "Competing for the future":

In the 1990s when the American business scenario was bleak, companies went on a cost-cutting rampage. During that period, Profs. Gary Hamel and C. K. Prahalad brought out their seminal book "Competing for the future" which became highly influential and changed the thinking of then American CEOs. They pointed out how top management of firms should look beyond immediate future and take steps to shape the industry future and remain market leaders. Their ideas can be summed up as follows:

i. From competing for market share, cutting costs through Business Process Reengineering techniques and transforming their own companies, CEOs should also compete for future opportunities, transform the industry as a whole through regenerating their strategic thinking.

ii. Instead of just sticking to old ideas and treating strategy as a static plan, they need to forget their past habits which are not relevant for the future and look beyond by developing long-term strategic outlook and vision.

iii. Strategy should be more than allocating resources to fit the opportunities. It has to stretch the resources and leverage them for higher returns.

iv. They have to move from competing within an existing industry structure for product leadership as a single entity, to rewriting the shape of the industry and its borders by working in coalition with partner organisations and also move on to the world stage.

With liberalisation and globalisation of the Indian economy from a closed economy where public sector was at commanding heights under a permit/ licence regime in the early 1990s, these guiding principles had profound impact on CEOs of India's large business houses, especially since late Prof. C. K. Prahalad became consultant to many of them.

15. Innovation strategy:

i. Before we move on to innovation strategy, let us briefly look at the meaning of creativity and innovation in organisational context. For our purpose, we can look at creativity as conceiving a new idea, something that is not known or in existence. Innovation stands for improving on existing ideas, products or services through newer ways of thinking and working. While organisations need both creative and innovative abilities, it is often thorough innovation which leads to practical application that they get early results. Creativity is often used in the field of Arts. The famous Austrian economist Joseph Schumpeter gave the idea of "creative destruction" as the inevitable way forward for companies and economy as a whole, to grow and stay relevant by discarding old ideas and adopting new ways.

ii. From the above discussions, we can see that firms need to innovate and keep changing things for the better. However, as a commercial proposition, they also have to analyse to what extent they will benefit from this innovation.

   •   Will this give competitive advantage to the firm?

   •   Can the firm sustain this competitive advantage to reap full benefits before it becomes commonplace practice in the industry?

- To what extent the firm can retain or appropriate the profits from innovation? Several examples can be cited on this question of appropriability vs. acceptability since the innovation will gain acceptance only when it reaches bulk of the customers. Apple Computers kept their operating system close to themselves and became the leader in the USA. On the other hand, while IBM made its operating system to all PC manufacturers and reaped enormous profits globally, their own PCs became unsustainable due to price competition from low-cost manufacturers and finally they sold off PC business to Lenovo.

- In today's information world, keeping anything proprietary is very difficult and company's innovative strategy becomes available to competitors very soon. Hence to ensure sustainability as well as appropriability for maximum profits, companies need to build in several innovative features and only when these are taken together, they will yield results. To replicate all these innovative key success factors together for the chosen segment, will be almost impossible for competitors even if they manage to copy one or two aspects of this innovative strategy. An example would once again be IKEA. The company built in several innovative features which can never be fully replicated like 1) huge stores outside city centres 2) unique shopping experience 3) price/utility equation 4) global sourcing including styling, design etc 5) unique flat packaging 6) transport and assembly by customer (DIY) at home etc.

3. Timing: Another important aspect of innovative strategy would be the timing of implementation. There are several advantages of being the "first mover".

- Increased market share in total industry and dominant position in the new market segment
- Consequently, greater profits
- Customer loyalty and new customer base
- Company image as an innovator

However, companies need to be careful about timing of market entry. Early introduction has certain risks:

- Markets/customers may not be ready to accept new product/marketing strategy
- Switching costs for the customers may be high
- Due to these, there is risk of losing investments made in R & D, product/market development etc.
- Invasion by a more nimble, astute competitor with greater resources who copies immediately and takes away the advantage, reducing the company effectively to a second mover.

Thus, it cuts both ways. But if firms do not respond to wake-up calls, they will end up losers and may even be driven out of business. Firms like Kodak and Nokia are often quoted as examples of such negligence in spite of having the necessary resources and technological leadership. Kodak had several patents for digital photography but never acted on them, trying to maximise their profits with their conventional films before it became too late. Same is the case with Nokia in spite of having technology for smart phones. India's Nano car from Tatas may be an example of wrong positioning and committing the strategic mistake of being "ahead of time".

All discussions above only indicate that companies need to be agile and have the necessary capability to gain market insight a well as be ahead in technology in today's world of products with short life cycles.

16. Corporate strategy:

i.   What we have discussed so far largely pertains to firms operating in one industry, offering one or a few products and services primarily to one market. As the firms grow, they get into multi-product, multi-market operations and they become corporations with many divisions and companies under them. Such corporations may be classified as under:

- Multi-divisional: operating within one market with several divisions each managing one or a few products/markets with a central corporate management

- Multi-national or multi-domestic, where firms operate in several markets, each firm in each country as a separate company

- International, where company has a central corporate management with branches/units in several countries/regions organised along a matrix structure

  These structures are based on the fundamental principle of differentiation and integration of corporate activities.

ii. Strategies for growth: Firms grow in size by increasing the scope of their activities as follows:

- Vertical scope: They increase their vertical scope by backward integration of getting into raw materials, components etc and/or increase their forward integration of moving from raw material/ component manufacture to complete products, servicing, financing etc.

- Geographical scope: Here they enter new regions, new countries.

- Product scope: They increase their product scope by diversifying into other industries, related or unrelated to existing products and markets.

iii. Global strategy: When a corporation gets into several countries apart from home country directly as an international company with a centralised corporate management, it becomes a global company. This offers certain distinct advantages like:

- Globalisation of customer preferences: Examples are Coca-Cola or Pepsi who have made soft drinks a global phenomenon. In our country, with the growth of IT industry, several people moved into high income brackets and became customers for international brands, especially for global luxury goods.

- Economies of scale: In capital-intensive industries, this offers economies of scale. Many processors of natural resources fall into this category, like oil companies, plastics manufacturers etc.

iv. Diversification: Companies diversify based on the following considerations:

Companies diversify into unrelated industries for following benefits:

- Higher growth opportunities when they get into new sunrise industries

- Increased profitability when they enter industries offering higher margins

- Risk reduction when they can reduce business risk by spreading it over different industries

However, companies are well advised to carry out a thorough study of the proposed industry to see whether they have necessary resources and capabilities to develop competitive advantage in that industry. Again, there are several examples of total corporate failure when they tried to diversify without a thorough study of the new industry requirements and their own capabilities.

v.   Functions of corporate management: The primary functions of corporate top management include:

- Formulate and manage corporate strategy by managing product/market portfolio through acquisitions, disinvestments, diversification and resource allocation
- Co-ordinate, monitor and control performance of constituent companies

These would call for leadership capabilities of the highest order.

17. Challenges facing strategy development:

From a simple one-liner "Make profits" through "Command and control" mode of functioning, strategy development has continuously been evolving reactively and pro-actively to changes in the external business environment. While Prof. Michael Porter's theory of competitive advantage and Profs. Hamel and Prahalad's and other thinkers' resource-based approach to strategy, have formed the basis for strategy making, there are newer challenges facing the mangers in the strategy process consisting of strategic analysis, choice and implementation, just to remind us that it is a dynamic process. Some of the major challenges are listed below:

i.   Need for nimble and agile responses to new challenges with ever-changing business environment

ii. Need for continuous environment scanning to spot "weak signals" and emerging trends to gain customer and market insights ahead of competition

iii. With Information and Communication Technologies (ICT) having changed the ways customers live and buy their requirements of products and services, the growing emphasis on network effects for developing and maintaining the highest levels of customer relationships. Examples are:

- Amazon as a one stop on-line shop for all customer needs

- Apple from I- tunes, I-pads, and I-phones and more

- Google as unquestioned leader as on-line search engine, related services and advertising platform

- Microsoft with Windows platform dominating all applications

- And onto Cloud Computing by giants like Amazon, Microsoft, IBM, Google etc

iv. Sophisticated financial techniques and measures to account for fulfilment of all stakeholder expectations, newer valuation tools and conformance to standards of ethical behaviour.

In order to direct the efforts of the organisation towards fulfillment of expectations of all stakeholders, a comprehensive performance measuring concept called Balanced Score Card is used. Under this, firms establish objectives, measures, targets and initiatives to fulfill firms' vision under four perspectives:

- Financial perspective

- Customer perspective

- Internal business processes perspective

- Learning and growth perspective

With increasing awareness among general and investing public, companies are resorting to newer measures to present their performance reports. Some of the major frameworks incorporating these measures are:

- ESG: Environmental, Social and Governance metrics for measuring a company's ability to create long term value for investors

- TPL: Triple Bottom Line accounting framework for measuring social, environmental and financial performance

v. Finally, there are the new emerging technologies of the digital world like Artificial Intelligence (AI), Internet of Things (IOT), 3-D Printing, Robotics, Block Chain etc. etc.

These have profoundly changed and will continue to change the organisational cultures, structures and strategies that have been covered in this booklet.

On top of the challenges listed here, as we are witnessing, the pandemic Covid 19 has really upended the old ways of doing business and it will take a while for organisations to adjust their ways of working in the emerging scenario. There is much talk of agility, resilience etc in management and economic studies these days. It is just overstating the fact that organisations need to be prepared for continuous major changes in the days to come to survive and prosper.

8. Taking a larger view:

would like to conclude this booklet with my own thinking on enlarging the vision and mission of business organisations beyond their traditional boundaries and stakeholders. From what we have seen so far on business strategy, we can understand that companies need to match their resources and capabilities with opportunities available in the market to meet the expectations of all stakeholders and make profits and add on to the wealth of shareholders. However, general public and governments largely look at business corporations with suspicion since they seem to be intent only on making more and more short-term profits without considering the requirements of other stakeholders and general public.

As we are witnessing, the Covid 19 pandemic has brought in innumerable hardships to most of the citizens while the super-rich and high-income groups of people have grown richer disproportionately. More than ever before, governments are saddled with the challenges faced by the society and to put the economies back on track towards achieving shared prosperity for all people.

With their market and money power, business organisations are uniquely placed to actively participate in this rebuilding exercise. It is high time large corporations took on this role by extending the boundaries and scope of their activities and lending a helping hand to the governments and thereby to rest of the population. They need to enlarge their vision and mission in letter and spirit and participate in any activity of their choice and competence. Making profits need not be the only bottom line.

Primary reference books

1. Study Materials for B-800: Foundations of Senior Management By the Open University Business School, UK

2. Marketing 3.0: From Products to Customers to the Human Spirit (2010) By Philip Kotler, Hermawan and Iwan Setiawan

3. Marketing Management: A South Asian Perspective (13th Edition- 2009) By Philip Kotler, Kevin Lane Keller, Abraham Koshy and Mithileshwar Jha

4. Strategic Brand Management: Building, Measuring and Managing Brand Equity (2nd Edition- 2007) By Kevin Lane Keller

5. Mastering Management 2.0: Your Single-Source Guide to Becoming a Master of Management By Financial Times: Edited by James Pickford (2004)

6. Organisational behaviour (11th Edition - 2006) By Stephen P. Robbins and Seema Sanghi

7. Key management ratios: The 100+ ratios every manager needs to know (Fourth edition- 2008) By Ciaran Walsh

8. Contemporary Strategy Analysis (Third Edition - 1998) By Robert M. Grant

Afterword

I started writing the booklet on Basics of Business Management and subsequent booklets covering each block by end of 2019. So far, I have completed four booklets and two more remain. The Covid 19 pandemic hit the world right through this period of end 2019, whole of 2020, 2021 and third and fourth waves are on us right now since January 2022. It has shaken the very basics of our lives to a great extent. As a consequence, whatever is written here has to be seen in this changed context. While all the basic and classic ideas presented here are equally applicable in the present circumstances, we need to modify the ways in which we apply them in the present context.

For example, work from home and online meetings have become the new norms in inter and intra office meetings involving white collar jobs. However, one can see a yearning as well as reluctance to get back to normalcy as soon as possible with abatement of the pandemic. Similarly, the phenomenal growth of online shopping has changed the ways in which products are promoted, stored, bought and delivered. These have given way to new business opportunities and have also led to the demise of many established ones. Integrated global supply chains are fraying at their ends to meet the supplies and demands from various parts of the world.

Driving all these is the relentless growth of the digital technologies. While this has brought in several advantages, it has also created many challenges. Navigating business in the digital world is the basic challenge faced by all companies and their managers.

With greater penetration of social media, people in all countries have become more aware of developments all over the world. As seen earlier, this has revolutionised the way people see and buy products and services. Brand loyalty based purely on premium image by multinational corporations (MNCs) is taking a beating with the emergence of "value for money" shift in consumer's minds. While more avenues for finance are available, pressures to control costs and offer robust profits to shareholders are proving to be great challenges in managing the finances of organisations.

Further, this has also brought in greater awareness among people on growing inequalities. It is an established fact that the rich, especially the very rich, have grown disproportionately rich and the poor, the bottom of the pyramid, have become poorer. Women empowerment as well as emerging groups like LGBT (lesbian, gay, bisexual and transgender) all need recognition and expect acceptance and opportunities available to others. Organisations cannot just stop at paying lip service to the concept of 'equal opportunity employer' but need to implement the same in letter and spirit.

In the current global political scenario, the so-called "superpowers" are flexing their muscles and are becoming more and more protective of their industries and territories. Emerging nations, having suffered suppression by them are also jostling for niche space more vigorously. A unipolar world that existed with the demise of Soviet Union is once again witnessing great rivalries between the two economic superpowers of USA and China. Both of them and Russia are vying to be the leader in the global context with financial, trade and military might and unbridled ambition for expanding their territories and spheres of influence. These conflicts have created great tension and flareup among them and other nations which have aligned with them all over the world. At the same time, threat of nuclear warfare by any indiscriminate ruler in any one of these countries hangs heavily in the air and the United Nations has been reduced to a mute spectator. These have led to authoritarian leaders in many countries and democratic values and freedom of thought and expression have been curtailed.

How true this has played out is being seen by the unexpected invasion of Ukraine by Russia, started in February 2022. This war has been dragging on till today causing much human misery and disturbing the whole world with prospects of massive hunger caused by sudden breakdown of supply chains. The comity of nations is getting fractured, and the threat of nuclear warfare appears real. As far as business and management fields are concerned, companies have gone back to drawing boards to rewrite their supply chain configurations even as they have just started implementing new supply chain strategies as a fallout of Covid 19. Once again, inequalities are rising and while new millionaires are springing up fast, millions of people are staring at abject poverty.

With the devastating blow delivered by Covid 19, governments have once again become the major economic engines in most of these nations. Giant technological corporations that dominate the digital world are fighting fiercely to protect their turfs as well as make inroads into others' domains. In the process, they are dictating the ways we, the people, live since our modern lives depend on them. Governments are finding it more and more difficult to rein them in due to their financial and market powers.

Most of the world is facing the reality of environmental degradation and the growing green movement to protect the globe for the present and future generations is gathering force.

All these have naturally affected all organisations' priorities, objectives, strategies etc.

Summing up, we can say that "business as usual" or old ways of doing things will not work anymore. New, innovative ways need to be found to meet these challenges constantly in this ever-changing scenario. However, I would like to emphasise that these basic, classic concepts and ideas still hold good, and we need to modify the ways we practise them. The basic purpose of these booklets is to expose the readers to all these classic concepts that have stood the test of time in a simple and concise manner so that they can start thinking and working out how to put them in practice in the current context.

A.S. Srinivasan   **October, 2022**

A.S. Srinivasan

A.S. Srinivasan holds a bachelor's degree in Mechanical Engineering (from the University of Madras), a Post Graduate Diploma in Plastics Engineering (D.I.I.T. from the Indian Institute of Technology, Bombay) and a Master's degree in Business Management (M.B.M. from the Asian Institute of Management, Manila, Philippines). He has participated in the Global Program for Management Development of the University of Michigan Business School.

Srinivasan has over 25 years of experience in industry and 15 years of experience in academics and consulting. His industry experience is primarily in the areas of Marketing and General Management in companies like TI Cycles, Aurofood, Pierce Leslie and Cutfast.

His last assignment was with Chennai Business School, a start up business school in Chennai, for over two years. As the first Dean of the school, he developed and implemented the curriculum for the post graduate program in management for the first batch. Prior to that, he was working with Institute for Financial Management and Research (IFMR), Chennai, for 8 years looking after the partnership with the Open University Business School (OUBS), UK in offering their Executive MBA in India. Apart from handling courses in the PGDM program of IFMR, he was actively involved in offering Management Development Programs (MDPs) to corporates and in consultancy assignments.

His current interests are in the areas of Management, Business, Economics etc. where he would like to keep himself updated with recent developments. He has taken to publishing blogs on these subjects for private circulation.

A.S. Srinivasan
1/3/4, "Srinivas", Third Main Road,
Besant Nagar, Chennai 600 090
Mobile: 91 98414 01721
Email: sansrini@gmail.com

Printed in Great Britain
by Amazon

42530021R00040